# DARK THREADS
## A GATHERING OF DARK FANTASY TALES

### DARK THREADS
#### VOLUME ONE

## KAT FARROW

LOREWEAVER PRESS

LoreWeaver Press, LLC

Cover art created by Kat Farrow with the aid of Midjourney generative AI

*The Withering*: Copyright © 2020 by Kat Farrow

*The Breath Borrower*: Copyright © 2020 by Kat Farrow

*Vapors of Misuse*: Copyright © 2022 by Kat Farrow

First Edition 2025

Paperback ISBN: 978-1-959123-09-5

eBook ISBN: 978-1-959123-08-8

# CONTENTS

# A NOTE ON CONTENT

The author writes in a wide variety of genres, including works for children.

Be advised that this is, indeed, a dark fantasy collection, and contains some content that might not be suitable for some readers.

This includes descriptions of violence, child abuse, and death, among other things.

If this collection is not your cup of tea, please disengage for your own wellbeing.

Sometimes the dark offers the only way forward.

TALE 1

# THE BREATH BORROWER

I slip through the window, quieter than the breath I seek.

A merchant this time with gurgling snores at the start of every inhale. The sound buzzes around the room as if a tired bee is trapped against a pane of glass.

Moonlight dims the purples and reds of the ornate rug beneath my feet. Extinguished candles, the thickness of my arm, tower upon the tables next to the carved wooden bed. A thin, embroidered bedcover stretches across the man's portly form.

Moving closer, I catch sight of his bed companion. A slight, younger man—if not a boy—his cheeks rich with peach fuzz. His breathing is deep and free from the incessant hum. The musky scent of mingled bodies emanates from them, blending with sweet wine and a lemony whiff of...

Glancing toward the solid pools of candle wax, I see the dry leafy remnants of Nightsinger. I stifle a grunt. Neither of them will be aware of me this night.

My silent footsteps end beside tapestry slippers and I stand listening to the buzz, hesitating. I know I will not enjoy this one, but the Receiver cannot wait.

Bending to a hands-breadth above the man's face, I focus, and match my breaths with his.

Two breaths. Three. Then, I have the rhythm. I open the space granted to me by the Great One. An extra pocket to store the air needed elsewhere. The grace of a third lung.

My chest expands. The fermented odor of the man's drink and drug is repulsive, not intoxicating. But it is what was requested. I pull it in deeply, watching the man's chest fall lower than before. It fails to rise for two of my own breaths, then returns to its previous vibrating hum.

I pull away with a last look at the companion, bare chest rising in a smooth, slow rhythm. His breath would have been sweeter, but I am not the one who chooses.

Returning to the window, I ease out onto a narrow ornamental ledge running the length of the brick building. I lower myself down and hang by my fingertips, the move difficult with the extra pressure in my chest. I drop to the balcony below, a huff of my own breath expelling with the landing.

Preparing to cross to the next balcony, my straps loosen and slip across my ribs. It had not been my night for Borrowing and in my rush to prepare for the assignment, I had failed to secure my wrappings tight enough. Crouching below the level of the railing, I reach inside my fitted tunic and tug at the cloth strips that bind my breasts. I know I should loose them and do away with the binding. Most of the other Borrowers do. It allows more space for the air. But it was so much easier to be a boy when I was young. It is a hard habit to break.

Cinching the straps tight, I twist my torso back and forth to make sure it stays snug. Satisfied, I peer over the top rail at the surrounding buildings. This four-story building is one of the tallest in this district and allows me a view of the entire street. The sweet shade of night dulls the white-washed walls, many dotted with flowering plants hanging outside shuttered or curtained windows. The swept cobbled streets are deserted and still, but for the breeze rustling the curtains and brushing the leaves of the plants.

Satisfied no eyes are about, I stand and gain the next balcony to access the adjacent roof. With sure steps I cross the curved roof tiles and head east, to the temple district.

A gibbous moon lights my way across the rooftops and provides deep shadows in the alleyways to hide me. Covered from head to toe in the dark gray hues of shadows, I am seldom seen on my assignments. Those that do glimpse me pretend they have not. I do not know if they realize who or what I am, or if they believe me to be just a thief.

I suppose I am, but a holy one... now.

I prefer the rooftops, but there are areas of the city where my weight creaks the roof beams, and I'd rather not join the inhabitants below. The air is sweeter here; the wind carrying away the faint stench that snakes along the tight streets and alleyways belonging to most of the city. Echoes of the night are softer, too. The scrapes and thumps less ominous. And the view; a blend of stone, tiled, and wooden roofs, with patches of thatch sprinkled throughout the poorer districts. All bathed in sleepy moonlight. Clean and peaceful in its deception.

The buildings grow farther apart as I move closer to the temple district. I leap with more force, rejoicing in the exertion and the breeze that blows through my thin clothing. The recent rains have left a light layer of moss across the roofs, and as my foot hits the shingles of the next roof, I slip.

Falling forward, I land on my forearms, protecting the breath in my chest. Fingers scrabbling against the slick wood to find purchase, I slide off to my thighs.

*Pay attention, Najidah.*

I inch myself toward the peak and sit for a moment, assessing the surrounding buildings. I spot a set of stairs leading down from a room behind a tavern. With care, I make my way to its roof, drop to the top landing and descend to gain the alleyways. Hopping down the last few steps, I startle a cat, finishing a meal of rat. The gray tabby growls at me.

The corner of my mouth tugs upward. There were never enough cats to keep the rat population down when I was young. My feet still bear the scars from bites of the wretched things.

"Sorry, little one. Good boy. You finish your meal."

My eyes widen and my right hand flies up to slap across my mouth. I dart furtive glances up and down the alley. Broken barrels and a few crates, but I discern no living thing but the cat. My shoulders drop and I fill my own lungs with a steadying breath. The scent of stale beer and souring cabbage tinge the air. All is silent but for the distant creaking of shutters and the skittering of rats and street dogs prowling.

I am grateful; for Breath Borrowers are Blessed and are not to speak.

Few of the temple's inhabitants are allowed to speak. The chanting of the Holy Ones will often echo through the stone hallways, but the priestesses are the only voices heard in speech. They talk to those who come to worship or seek aid. They speak with each other and give assignments to the Holy Ones and the monks. And they speak to us, though that is during our training.

A growl emanates near my feet again. I meet the glowing eyes of the tabby, teeth sunk deep into the gray fur of its prey. My hand drops and I take a step back. Another glance up and around, then I resume my task with more speed than before.

There are fewer backstreets in this district, but I take them when I can. Street lamps run along the main thoroughfares, their burning oil creating patches of glowing gold, but strengthening the shadows between. The changing light patterns are harsh on my night vision, so I avoid them while I can.

Rounding a corner, I catch the sound of footfalls echoing through the streets ahead. The curfew has been less stringent these days, but it is unusual for someone to be openly striding about. I pause, listening as the hard thud of boots on stones become louder. The flickering of a shape passing a lamp plays against the far wall. I pull myself into the shadows.

A stout man strides out across the next intersection.

He pauses in the middle of the crossroads, looking up and down the streets. He turns in my direction and I sink into the dark of an alcove.

I peer around the edge of the bricks, watching. The man walks down the very middle of the road as if he belongs there. But I can see a ragged hem on the long brown coat he wears, even in the warmer weather. Too disheveled to fit this district.

There is something about his shape and movement that is familiar. A hitch in his step and his constant tugging at the wide brim of his dark hat. He passes a light and I glimpse his face.

Genid. A true thief and a mean one.

*What is one of the Thief Lord's underlings doing so close to the temples?*

He is swift tonight, despite his bulk, with heavy determined steps. He runs his hand through his mangy reddish beard, something I've only seen him do when nervous. When he draws near, I pull my head back, pressing my body hard into the cool bricks. Clenching my fists, I will myself to become part of the darkness surrounding me.

It has been years and he may no longer recognize me; but then, he thinks I'm dead. I'd rather not disappoint him.

Closing my eyes, I feel the breeze of his passing. The stench of liquor and rancid meat lingers from his coarse breath and clothes. I count his steps as they fade, and peer out of my alcove to watch him turn a corner further down the street. Taking a deep breath, I feel the extra pressure in my chest.

*I have someplace to be.*

I turn my back on a piece of my past, the one in which I bore a different name: Calla. I blink hard as the memories tease at my thoughts and swallow the sharp bitterness rising in my throat, then move faster, hoping it will help push the thoughts back into their bleak corner.

Turning down the street the thief came from, I continue until the narrow, cobbled streets open upon a wider avenue. The Great One's temple is at the end. I pause, resting in a shadow. The extra breath I hold leaves less room for my own and my swift movements, combined with the sight of Genid, have left me winded.

I look to the west tower of the temple and see the pendulum lantern swinging in the window. After a few passes, the color changes from pale yellow to dark orange. A signal that time is running out.

I push on down the street and past the temple's elaborate carved facade to the back entrance, the one the poor and desperate use. Those who fall back on the forgotten ways when things go horribly wrong. The one I had come to years ago.

A large muscled monk is waiting for me, blocking the heavy wooden door. He doesn't look like he belongs in the robes. The seams of the dark-brown homespun stretch taut across his shoulders. I do not know his name, though I have seen him many times. From the look he gives me, I know he does not care to know mine. The monks are never civil toward Borrowers. They think we are an abomination and not Blessed.

The monk swings open the door and the flickering

light from the hall candles illuminates the threshold with its one carved symbol. The Breath of Life.

The impatient monk grunts, the most sound his vows allow, and waves me in toward the left corridor, though I know the way.

A warm, steady light spills out the third doorway onto the slab floor of the hall. I enter to see a middle-aged woman lying on the high stone table as if in offering to the Great One. The attending priestess motions me forward, then begins chanting her prayers.

Approaching, I notice droplets of sweat surrounding the supine woman's hairline. A few joining into rivulets and rolling down her placid skin to drip off her ear to the damp sheet she lies upon.

Her breath is thin, thinner than the drab threadbare clothing covering her shivering form. I smell the blood from her cracked and broken ribs and bend down low, a kiss away, not wanting any of the gift to escape.

I wait. The woman's breath is so fretful it is difficult to find its rhythm. When I have it, I open the third pocket of air and breathe it slowly into her damaged lungs. A second priestess pulls me away as soon as I am done. I stand against the wall, trembling a little as I watch the Holy Ones enter, swinging their incense.

They pace in complex circles, their pale gray robes offering a soft swooshing against the stone floor. Their low chanting is deep and rhythmic. The sharp pine-like scents of frankincense and rosemary fill the room as they weave around the table. The two priestesses lay their hands upon the woman, waiting for the remnants of the alcohol and drug in the air I carried to numb her.

The woman's breath strengthens—until they move the bones back into place. Then the breath I brought expunges from her in shaky cries. Her own breaths return, though. Shallow at first, then growing deeper. As I watch, her pallor softens to shades of the living. My own two lungs fill and I sigh.

A shoulder tap pulls my attention and the large monk from the entrance motions me away. He escorts me down the right corridor to the assignment room. Odd, as I am often only given one assignment a week, if that, but the old cleric is still there. His sagging jowls mimic his slouchy, worn robes. The stack of paperwork beside him seems to have grown, not diminished in the hour since my last assignment.

I shift my feet to gain his attention. He flicks his hand at me to be still. A few moments later, his stern brown eyes look up to meet mine. Unblinking, he hands me a folded assignment sheet, then his eyes return to his work.

My name is written upon the thin linen leaf in the cleric's neat quill. The one the High Priestess gave me when the temple took me in. Najidah. She told me it means "to assist" in the old language. I prefer this name to the one I left behind, but I wish I could have been the one to choose it.

Unfolding it, I read the names of the Giver and Receiver. My breath catches and my mouth falls open. I look back at the cleric, hoping to catch his attention again. But he is focused on his stack of paperwork. I look back at the names, a word forming on my tongue. But before a sound slips past my tongue again this night, the large monk is tapping my shoulder once more and gestures me out. I glance again at the cleric, but to him I might as well be the air I carry.

In a haze, I follow the burly monk to the entrance. He ushers me through, and the thud of the door closing behind me echoes through the empty streets. The sound runs a shiver across my skin, even in the early summer heat. I glance at the paper again, but it is too dark for me to read. I know what it says, even if I don't want to believe it.

Turning back to the dark door, my eyes fall to the threshold. There is not enough light to see the holy symbol, but for a moment—

I blink hard to dispel the image and give my head a shake.

*There is no blood, just a memory.*

Crinkled edges of the sheet stab into my palm. Relaxing my clenched fists, I smooth the sheet against my thigh. Folding it, I tuck it into a pocket and turn to head toward my first destination.

I have been to the palace once before, but then it was to deliver a breath, not to take one. Our contacts there will know a Borrower will be coming, but uncertainty tugs at my mind as to where their true loyalties will lie.

My unease preoccupies me as I pass through the city. I am going faster than I should and make novice mistakes as I cross the rooftops. A dog catches sight of me as I pass overhead. It gives a shrill bark of alarm and I scramble up the tiles out of sight when I land. I fail to notice the rich, earthy scent and glowing red embers of a man smoking on a balcony until I pass over his head.

I decide to stick to the ground as I near the palace, giving up my rooftops to avoid notice by the tower guards. The city has been peaceful as of late, and the night guards of the palace are few. But I'd rather not risk it.

Just outside the palace's southern wall, I wait in a cusp of darkness for the signal. An occasional guard comes and goes through a small open gateway, and I sink a little deeper into the waning night. A blue lantern flashes twice in the turret window above. A pause, then twice more. I move through the doorway and across the small yard to an unobtrusive servant door. I repeat the light pattern in knocks. The door opens and I slip through.

The contact will not meet my eye; they seldom do. It is an older woman; her face pinched and sour. Her light blue dress and stained white smock are a mark of the kitchen staff. I follow her down a passageway, then turn left up a staircase. The woman continues on her own way with flapping footsteps echoing down the hall.

All Borrowers memorize a map of the palace, in case we are needed in an emergency. I have not trod this particular hallway, but a few of our silent feet have. I turn down a marbled hallway, my steps cushioned by rugs patterned with peacock feathers, and pass through a balcony corridor, its shutters flung wide to the night breeze. Turning once more, I see my destination at the far end.

The door is closed and unguarded. A magnolia tree is carved into its wood and painted a pale green and pink that compliments the surrounding white marble. Oil lamps cast their golden glow from wall niches between the door and its neighboring doorways. I pause, listening. My own breath is all that I hear. I use the door to the right instead of the magnolia one, and pass into the nursemaid's chamber. Empty and dark, as I expected.

I cross the room to peer through the open balcony doors. Curtains brush across my cheeks with the slight breeze as I gaze at the tranquil palace grounds. The balcony runs along the wall to the left, so close to the next balcony, a short jump is all that is needed. The cool shade of a cloud passes the bright moon and then I am standing at the edge of the other room's balcony door, looking through its curtain. Quiet, dark, and still. Empty but for the small figure upon the bed.

Closing my eyes, my hand moves across the pocket holding the folded paper, as if my fingertips could read the names on their own. I pull a deep breath and open my eyes. Time is a limited gift and I must hurry. I loose my feet from the heavy hold the balcony floor has gained and cross the room to the narrow bed.

Sefan, the youngest prince, will be five in a few weeks. He is tiny and frail, tucked under many layers of the softest linens, even in the late summer balm. Small gold bowls of myrrh rest on either side of his pillow, and a symbol of healing is drawn upon his forehead in indigo and white chalk.

His breath is soft and shallow. Bending over him, I smell traces of cardamom and cedar. Wards to guard his health. I know of his trials. Everyone does.

My eyes focus on an eyelash resting on his pale

cheek. I squelch the urge to brush it away, as I would have with my younger siblings.

I regard the whole of the young prince's heart-shaped face. The thick dark lashes, short ebony curls and a freckle a finger-width away from the outer corner of his eye. Just like Lendi.

My breath stops.

I have never seen the prince from this close. Never realized how much he looked like my younger brother. Lendi was almost four when his undernourished body was crushed by the foot of the Thief Lord.

I step back and force in a shaky breath. The Thief Lord, Hedred, is the other name on my assignment sheet.

I retreat further from the prince and set to a slow stride across the room's pale green carpet. Its softness pulls at my feet until I am standing still.

*Why would the High Priestess assign this task to me?*

I glance back at the sleeping prince, then close my eyes.

*I must trust her. She saved me.*

I breathe deeply, seven times. Calmer now, I open my eyes and approach the young prince once again.

*I must do as assigned. All will be well.*

I reach the bed and bend down, hovering so close I can feel the heat of his skin. His breaths are so shallow they are hard to grasp. I realize I will need to take more than one.

At last I match the rhythm and open the space. I take two, my third lung still not quite full, but I dare not take more.

I wait, watching the prince's chest. But three of my own breaths and his do not return.

A heavy pounding grows against the constraint in my chest.

*Breathe.*

One more of my breaths and none of his.

I lean in, all but touching his lips, and return a breath. I watch his small chest.

Nothing.

Return the second breath.

*Please.*

Nothing. It is almost too long.

I look at the small face, so much like Lendi. My eyes return to his chest.

Still nothing.

The corners of my eyes prickle. I turn to the sweet face again and give some of my own breath, a quarter breath for Sefan's small lungs.

I wait and listen, turning my ear to his small mouth.

Three of my own shallow breaths and a small gasp seeps from the prince's thin lips. I watch his chest rise a little, fall, then rise again. I watch for a dozen of my own breaths and the movement continues.

Retreating a few steps, I wait to make sure the rhythm doesn't falter.

I wipe at a dampness by my eyes and when my hand falls back to my side it brushes against the pocket with the assignment sheet.

*I cannot fail the High Priestess.*

I watch the sleeping child, then find myself turning

back toward the window. A few steps and my feet slow; I turn and walk to the door instead.

I place my hand upon the cool wood. The light from the hall seeps under the door a few inches, illuminating the white marble and the tips of my dark shoes. No shadows play in it. I open the door and leave the palace same way I came.

Once clear of the wall, I find my feet running until I come to the safety of alleyways. I stop and lean against a building, aging plaster cracking from my weight. My lungs ache and I cannot seem to draw in enough air to fill them.

I could return to the temple. Try asking for another name. But the heavily jowled monk would not help, even if he could. I do not know of another breath to give, nor how the priestesses choose.

If there had been another choice, I would not have been sent where I was. The task must be completed. Time is short and I am one of the Blessed. Chosen.

The Thief Lord would not have gone to the temple for aid. He would have the priestesses go to him. The High Priestess, herself, may be there. Perhaps she will tell me what can be done.

My feet know the way and start before my thoughts have settled. I stick to the ground, the crushing weight of my heart leaving my balance too askew for jumping rooftops. It is a part of the city I have avoided since I was twelve.

The Chink. The place and people that took the lives of my sister and brother. And meant to take mine.

My sister, Niya, had starved herself. A year younger

than I, she had been much prettier beneath the grime. Hedred and his men noticed before I did. They had taken her while I was away searching for food. They took her twice. Only twice. And then she stopped eating. I did not realize it at first. I thought she was just giving extra to Lendi. He was so small, and we both wanted him to grow stronger. To have a chance. When I noticed just how thin Niya had become, it was too late. She no longer wanted food.

Less than a year later, returning to the Chink with a prized half apple tucked into my sleeve for Lendi, I came upon a nervous crowd. I could hear Hedred's bellows coming from its center, but could not discern the cause. My thin frame slipped through the hoard and I saw the Thief Lord stomping around a pile of rags. He was calling out about how thieving from his table would not be tolerated. His henchmen chuckled and cheered as the Thief Lord kicked the pile of rags in my direction. A pale thin arm flung out from the filthy cloth and my mind slowly registered the bundle was my brother.

A cry started in my throat, but stopped as Hedred's massive boot landed in the middle of Lendi's body. The crunch of bones echoing off the buildings.

My cry broke free into a high-piercing scream. It drew the Thief Lord's attention and through streaming tears I saw the people around me part and the massive man appear. He stood laughing, then slapped me hard against the side of my cheek. I fell back, my feet flying out from under me. Before I could grasp my surroundings, he was dragging me by my arm, almost pulling it out of its socket. He lifted me high and plunged me into a cistern, pushing me down to drown.

But, I didn't. My own two lungs filled with putrid water, but I did not die. After Hedred released his grip and his cohorts stopped thumping the barrel's wooden sides, the water stilled. I counted to twenty and timidly rose to break the surface. The last of the crowd was dissipating. The Thief Lord and his men were disappearing down the Hole.

I pulled myself up and let the foul liquid pour out of my mouth as I leaned over the edge. Gasping, as air filled my lungs, I turned toward Lendi's broken body. My vision was still blurry from the slap, but I saw his hand twitch. I climbed free of my watery coffin and made my way to him. He looked up at me, his lips trembling as they tried to form a smile. I fell to my knees and stroked his dark curls.

In a hissing whisper, he said, "Calla... take.... temple..."

A small mist of blood flecked his lips from the effort. I knew he was too broken for the temple to fix. But it was his last wish. One I had ignored when Niya had lain dying in my arms, a speck of hope playing in her dull eyes.

My fears of seeking help would not chain me this time. They had left me for dead. There would be no risk of reprisal.

I rose, and the rush of blood pounding in my injured head caused me to nearly fall on top of Lendi. I steadied and struggled to lift him up, my shoulder aching. After almost dropping him, I clutched his shirt and drug him through the filthy streets the two miles to the temple. Almost blind from the pain in my head, and heedless of my sorrow, I groped along the stone wall until I touched wood and pounded. The high priestess herself answered the door, and I fell across the threshold, still wet and clutching Lendi's bloody and lifeless body.

Days passed before I stayed conscious for more than a few minutes. When the High Priestess questioned me about not drowning, they examined me further and discovered I had been Blessed with the grace of a third lung. I didn't feel Blessed; I felt broken. As broken as Lendi's small body. The priestesses offered me a new life, one I would have lost long before now. And with it, I have helped so many.

Approaching the Chink, the streets narrow and become crowded with debris. I can feel unseen eyes following my movements through the shadows the closer I get. There is no reason to hide here. Everything is seen by someone, so I move from the edges to the center of the narrowing lane.

My pace is quicker than I want, but my feet are moving of their own accord. I still do not know what I will do when I get there. I have brought no breath to give. None but my own and I do not want to give it. Not to him.

I come to a place where two worn wood and stone buildings stand side by side, but staggered. From certain angles they appear to overlap, but there is a gap, the Chink itself. It is just wide enough for a cart and stays narrow for the depth of the buildings.

The space that opens beyond isn't much wider,

framed by the backs of mills and warehouses. Filled with hovels and stalls built on top of each other, they share walls and roofs. Some two and three-storied ones have balconies made from broken bits of plank that give way with a wrong step. Laundry is strung between these upper floors, always reeking of smoke and refuse.

Night breezes have cleaned the air as much as it can. The damp and rot are not as prevalent. The tang of urine and retching are still there. Always.

It is the early hours now. The creeping of the coming dawn tinging the tops of the surrounding buildings a pale gray. Snuffling noises and the rustle of clothing echo off the outer walls. A few people are still about, drinking and making bargains. More than usual, though. Tight little clusters with an abruptness to their whispers. They watch me as I make my way to the center of the Chink, to a larger open space just outside the Hole.

A specter of pain flashes across my cheekbone when I see the cistern that I drowned in before pulling my dying brother's body away. Noise and movement ahead pull my attention away from the memories creeping in. Several shadowy figures are moving in and out of the open corridor leading to my destination.

I wish for my feet to slow, but they continue on at a steady pace. They know their duty and ignore the sourness building in my stomach. I turn down the corridor, pretending not to see the mixed expressions of those I pass. Raised eyebrows or curled lips by the few who think they recognize me; a glimmer of hope in tear-stained eyes by those who don't.

The corridor slopes downward, under the buildings

that surround the Chink. I turn a corner and see a well-lit room ahead. A soft chanting by the Holy Ones echoes toward me. It must be a serious illness or injury for them to be here. I have never seen them outside the temple.

My deep dread has finally reigned in my feet and I slow as I step into the circle of light. The incense cannot hide the scents of unclean. To me, they are as intimate as the smell of blood in this place.

He is there. The one whose name has not crossed by lips in more than a decade. The High Priestess herself attends to him. I suspected this, but it does not stop my partially empty lungs from aching. I cannot fail her. Even for him.

His dais in this den of thieves now holds a makeshift bed instead of his massive, wooden mockery throne. Crates and casks support thick planks, but still they bow. He is such a large man, perhaps four or more of me.

I falter with this realization. Even with a full third lung, all my breath will not fill his. I watch the High Priestess pacing at the head of his bed, chanting softly. She glances at me, an odd look in her eye, and gives a subtle nod.

My jaw slackens. *She knows.* She knows I failed to bring the breath. Planned for this. Counted on this.

*What does she mean for me to do?*

The Thief Lord funds the temple as much as or more than the crown. They cannot want me to fail. Or is that why I was chosen? Because I come from this place and they know I still have a grudge deep within my heart.

I have been standing a pace within the circle of light for too long. His gathered minions are murmuring.

Staring at me. I catch sight of Genid, but his focus is solely on the Thief Lord.

The chanting grows louder and the Holy Ones emerge from a doorway on the left. A line of nine, swinging their sharp pine incense to fight the decay, their pale gray robes bright against the gloom of this place.

They walk close behind me. Close enough I step forward, nearer the makeshift bed. But my feet are heavy now and no longer want to move. The smoking circle tightens, squeezing me in closer to my destination. Another priestess has emerged and makes signs with aromatic oils upon the Thief Lord's arms and forehead.

I take another step closer, knowing I must. The High Priestess circles opposite of the Holy Ones and when she comes to me, she takes my hand to lead me to my place. I take a fleeting glance at her, hoping for clues. Does she expect me to give the last of my own breath?

We stop beside the prone man. With a gentle squeeze from the priestess's hand, I realize there is something between our palms. Something small and hard. I meet her eyes and there is a sharpness I have never seen. She squeezes my hand again, then gently lets go so that I enfold the small object with my fingers.

A smooth glass cylinder, its tapered shape my fingers recognize. I know what she asks of me now and it will be my own death. But it will be the Thief Lord's as well.

Letting the practice and routine of hundreds of Borrowings take over, I move close, taking my position. I watch the labored rise and fall of the man's breath. Worry had too consumed me to notice his condition until now. The normally reddish complexion of the man is yellow and clammy. His long auburn hair and beard, which he kept oiled and preened, are now unkempt and drenched in sweat. His scarred torso is wrapped in blood-stained rags. Just above his belt, the red liquid soaks through and drips along the plank seams to pool upon the filthy floor. I do not think he is long for this world, even without my assistance.

I regard the High Priestess for a moment, but she takes no notice, continuing her chanting. My unspoken assignment has been given. I take a deep breath, then turn my head and cover my mouth to cough. My hand trembles around the cold glass, but I crush the ampoule in my fist and breathe in. It burns instantly. A strong poison for a large man.

Bending down close to this thief of life, I hold my breath, my lungs burning as if licked by flames. I catch his stuttering rhythm and exhale into his next breath. I exude every spark of the invisible fire then step back gasping.

I cannot take in enough air. The damage is too great. Memories of the putrid water of the cistern flood through me and I stumble back, breaking through the path of circling Holy Ones.

I try to draw breath again, but it finds nowhere to go. Body shaking, I continue stepping backward, hoping to find the steadying force of the Hole's wall. Instead, my elbow is grasped by a large, firm hand. I look up, trying to focus, the edges of my vision blurring. It is the muscular monk again. He guides my faltering steps out of the room. There is a murmur of voices rising above the chanting behind us, but still he pulls me up the corridor. Its shadows darken my vision even more. Head aching with every movement, the noise is now muffled by my pounding heart. I stumble so often the monk is all but dragging me by the time we meet the street.

He pulls me further away from the entrance to the Hole and pushes me onto an empty cask. He tosses something soft upon my lap and bends down next to my ear. In a deep voice, he says, "For the life of my mother." Then walks away.

I try in vain to pull more air, like a drunk trying to suck the last drop of liquor from his jug. A shadow passes me and a cool hand cups my fevered cheek. In my blurred haze, I see a hooded face. I squint hard and recognize it. She is a Borrower as well, even younger than I.

She bends down, a kiss away, and exhales a cool sweet breath into my third lung. My empty lung that I had been too panicked to remember.

*Breathe.*

It tingles. A cool tingle that tempers the burning within. I gasp a deeper breath with the expanded lung. I try to hold the breath as long as I can to absorb whatever properties the gift is imbued with. My body shakes as it starves for more air. Finally, I exhale and take several deep, quavering breaths.

I concentrate on my third lung, thankful for my years of training to use it. Try to convince my mind to use only it and not my other heavy, useless ones.

The throbbing sound in my ears lessens and I can hear the cries and wails of mourning and anger echoing from the corridor I was pulled from. I look toward the commotion, but the other Borrower is there, blocking my view, or perhaps me from the view of others.

Her back is to me. After a few more breaths, I reach out and touch her arm gently. She doesn't turn. She fidgets with something inside her robe and then her hand thrusts backward toward me, gripping a small leather bag and a folded paper.

I take them. The bag is heavy with the weight of coins. After blinking tears from my slowly clearing eyes, I read the note in the pale light of the gaining day. It is in a different hand than my assignments. Seven words.

Leave City. Do Not Return. Thank You.

The other Borrower has turned to face me now. She points at the soft, brown fabric on my lap, and I recognize it now as a traveling cloak. I look up and see her hand outstretched. I take it and she pulls me up.

She releases me, and I am unsteady. My head is still clearing, my body covered in sweat as it expunges the poison. I am weak, with only one lung to move by, but I know I must. The outcry is getting louder and people are running past us now.

She holds out her hand again, a fist this time clutching something small. I reach out and she drops two more small ampoules into my palm. The tapered tips of each dipped in gold to indicate they are medicinal.

She gives me a tight-lipped smile, then leans in to kiss my cheek. She brushes past me, uttering, "For my family."

I place the vials in a pocket and pull the cloak over

my shoulders. I turn and follow the Borrower from a distance. Not to pursue her, but to leave the Chink. Forever this time. Every step is fragile and slow, my balance and sight gaining bit by bit. I pause now and then with my hand on a wall, steadying my still spinning head. My thoughts split between breathing and moving to the edge of the city.

I do not know if the ampoules will be enough to heal my damaged lungs. I may only be left with my third one, and life will be slower. Without rooftops. Once I make it out of the city, I do not know where I will go or what I will do. The two lives I have known are gone. I will become something and someone else. With a new name.

*This time, one of my choosing.*

TALE 2

# THE WITHERING

Cold singed Neela's flesh as she pinched the thin hard carapace of the effigy, making sure it was a solid object in this place of shadow and thought. Bone white and smooth, the oval was just larger than her face, with a slight bulge for a nose and two rectangular slits for eyes.

She took it from the chicosk spirit's outstretched hand. It varied from the one the chicosk wore over its face, but that was its own. Over time, the mask would have molded itself to the spirit's desire. Why that desire would be the face of King Jaluduth, one side melting in folds like the side of a spent candle, she could not guess. But the unsettling sight distracted her from the rest of her Underland guide's vague arthropodic shape.

Neela glanced up at the towering figure, its head nearly brushing the top of the tunnel. It gave a slow nod, encouraging her to place the mask over her face. The slight movement caused the tiny skeletal body dangling below the chin of her guide's mask to tinkle like hollow wooden chimes.

The mask she held had no skeletal body attached. She wasn't sure if it would grow one after she put it on, or if a visitor's mask never did. Her studies had found no record of seekers for several centuries, and the accounts of those who had gone before were vague about far too many things.

There was no ribbon or strap to attach to the mask. Puzzled, she held it up over her face and felt a slight pressure, as if she had dunked her face into water. The mask stuck. She could feel the cold brushing her skin, but the mask itself hovered a finger-width above her flesh. Hooking her thumb under the edge, she tugged. It would not come off and might not until she left the Underland. If she left.

Looking back up at the chicosk, she heard a tinkling from below her own chin. Her thin fingers brushed at the bottom of the mask but felt only the dry, chill air of the passageway. Focusing on the chicosk, she realized the mask altered her vision. The guide's shape had become more solid and she could clearly see its two long, multi-jointed arms and four legs. Its defined appearance was both more and less comforting than the dark, amorphous shape it had been.

Gaining her attention, it motioned her to follow. As soon as it turned, its body glowed, illuminating the dark passage in a soft blue light.

Neela dug her hands deep into her cloak pockets, touching the small objects they contained. Their familiarity comforted her as she watched the rippling movements of the chicosk moving further ahead. With a deep breath, she freed her feet from the soft ash and sand of the tunnel floor and followed. This is why she had come. To seek answers. To seek help for her dying world.

The chicosk moved steadily, turning its head to check on her progress now and then. The soft glow it created lit carved reliefs on the walls as it passed. Neela recognized many of the archaic symbols from her studies, several of which had defied translation over the centuries. Intricate patterns interspersed the symbols, complex versions of the prints used on the robes of the priests and royal family.

The chicosk's legs dipped in and out of the thick, sandy ash in silence. Its dangling bones tinkling only when it turned toward her. Neela's own bones clinked with every step, and every booted footfall made the slight shushing of sand passing through an hourglass.

As a child, Neela's grandmother had told her stories of the Underland. The place where thoughts were kept when not being used. Dreams, nightmares, inspirations, dread. They came and went as needed, but some became stuck or buried, forever lost to those who believed they had created them.

The chicosk guarded and cared for them. But there were other things in the Underland. Things that fed off the thoughts as much as tended them.

The legends told of a few brave souls who ventured into the Underland, seeking answers or lost knowledge. Those who returned had only sparse memories of the place and only received part of what they had been searching for. Neela had spent the past seven years combing the old scrolls for information to verify these legends. Long before she had the need of it. Before the deaths began.

Her people were starving, but it wasn't for lack of food. Something had changed in the plants. Or the soil. Or the water. It didn't matter how much you ate; you were never satiated. You never gained weight. Children never grew. Your body lost its ability to heal. And then, you began to Wither.

It spared no one, but affected some more quickly. It was even said the royal family lay Withering. None had seen the king himself for over a year.

Neela had lost friends and family. Her grandmother, hale and hardy less than three years ago, was now a shade away from death. Neela herself had not felt the full brunt of the Withering. Yet. She still had strength and a sharp mind. Still had more flesh on her bones than most of the population. She didn't know why...unless it was for this.

Her chicosk guide stopped as the tunnel opened upon a large vestibule. A glowing mist illuminated the carved stone room, circling far above. A dozen passage entrances lined its circular walls, and above each entrance was a symbol.

This was one detail which had been consistent in the recollections of those who had returned. Neela was to choose the one she believed would take her to her desire. She had not expected a different chicosk to be waiting in each entrance. A new guide for whichever way she chose.

Neela brushed a lank strand of light brown hair that had fallen across her mask's eye slits. She tried not to grimace as she felt several hairs come free to drift down to the ground.

Moving away from her first guide, she circled the room, reading each symbol. She was grateful she had spent so much time with the scrolls and polymaths. The symbols were in an ancient script. Only one gave her trouble.

*Future*
*Past*
*The Way of Light*
*The Way of Dark*
*Life*
*Death*
*The Way of Giving*
*The Way of Taking*
*Spirit*
*Flesh*
*Thought*

The last symbol looked like a combination of the glyphs for Nature and Imagination. She thought it might be an ancient glyph for *Magic*, but that didn't seem quite right.

In her studies, she had tracked down recollections from nine of the doors, but what they held now may have changed. Her quest was for something that had not been in those passages then. But there was no way to be sure now.

Neela moved to the center of the room, closed her eyes, and slowly turned. There was a light, woody scent that seemed to mix with the vestibule's musty air.

She stopped where the scent was strongest and

opened her eyes. The doorway with the unknown symbol was before her. She examined the chicosk guide looming just inside the passage.

Its dark brown mask was egg-shaped and the size of her whole torso. Deep, bark-like ridges ran horizontally, with inverted triangles as eye slots, roughly chiseled. The tiny skeletal body dangling from its mask's chin appeared to be made of sticks. It glowed less than the first guide and appeared to have twice as many legs disappearing into the shadows of the tunnel.

Skin prickling, Neela took a hesitant step, then stopped. She had one chance. She sunk her hands deep into the pockets of her cloak, turned and circled the room again, closer to each door.

Her fingertips passed over the objects she had brought. A small, seven-pointed bronze star, a silver coin, a thin glass vial of poisoned wine, a tiny corked pot of honey, a zeluu nut, a carved wooden bead, a palm-sized sack of barley grain, and a braided strand of her and her grandmother's hair. She had already given a gold coin to the first chicosk, to allow her passage into the Underland. She hoped the remaining items would be enough to achieve her goal.

When she again passed the doorway with the rough masked chicosk, her fingers brushed upon the zeluu nut; its smooth, oblong shell had turned ice cold.

Pausing, Neela turned to face the guide again. She pulled her hand from her pocket and held the nut out on her open palm. The chicosk's legs shuffled, but the mask remained still.

The strange Nature + Imagination symbol it would be then.

With a slow, silent breath, she moved closer to her new guide. She held the nut out an arm's length away from the silent being. Black, spider-legged fingers reached out and grabbed the small nut. The mask nodded, stick bones clicking, then the chicosk's body rippled and turned, its glow brightening to a pale gold as it moved down the passage.

The ground grew damp and soft under Neela's feet as she followed. A heavy mist appeared low on the floor, pulling up in wispy curls with each step of her guide.

This tunnel did not have the carvings of the first. Deeply grooved, it looked as if long claws had run the length of it. Like the mask of its chicosk keeper.

The ground grew bumpy, as if disturbed by the roots of trees. But the mist hid whatever it was, and Neela kept tripping, causing her dangling bones to clink and jingle. Ahead, a brighter glow illuminated the bobbing silhouette of the chicosk. A woody scent flooded her senses and her skin felt a slight breeze tinged with moisture.

The tunnel ended and opened into an immense cavern containing an underground forest. A soft blueish light filtered down from high above a dense canopy. Purple and green glow-snails left streaks upon tree trunks, and small balls of colored light darted like fire-flies around the overgrown foliage. Glowing fungus dotted the misty ground, and there were bushes with leaves longer than Neela's arm, bearing black flowers the size of her face. The breeze rustled leaves, but the odd forest had no sounds of birds or small animals.

Captivated, her eyes darted around the strange sights. Neela had read no descriptions of this place. She wondered if she would have been able to see any of it without her mask. She watched the path of two glowing spheres twisting around each other, then plummeting into a bush. Turning to seek others, she realized her chicosk guide was nowhere to be seen.

She was alone.

Recollections of the other passages taken had spoken of rooms with small doors, tables with objects to choose from, or a being to ask a question of. Here, there was no sign of the direction she had come from. No definite path to follow. No objects to choose from. Nor anyone to ask.

Her shoulders sagged, and a small sound of sorrow escaped her in a sigh. She pulled the braid of hair from her pocket and ran her fingers over the bumpy strands, taking deep, slow breaths. Calmer, she examined her surroundings more closely. She could see there was indeed no path to where she stood. No broken branches or bent leaves. The mists clung low against the ground, preventing her from seeing any footprints.

She crouched down and tried waving the mists back away from her feet, but the curls her hand movement created arched back and poised themselves like snakes about to attack. Pulling her arms in close, she slowly stood. The mists settled back down to their quiet swirling. She took a hesitant step and met no resistance from it.

She took another, then a sound made her jump, setting her bones tinkling. It was like the hoot of an owl, but very low and deep. She strained her ears listening as it echoed oddly, bouncing through the dense foliage.

The forest fell silent but for the light rustling of leaves, and she took another step. Then a bright orange dragonfly buzzed past her ear. It buzzed back and circled her, finally coming to hover a finger-width away from the nose bump of the mask. She went nearly cross-eyed, staring at its bulbous black orbs as it examined her. It was enormous, its body longer than the length of her forearm. The creature's wings beat a cold draft that whistled through her eye slits, making her blink.

It retreated a few feet and hovered. Neela took a step toward it. The dragonfly reversed its flight and flew a short distance, but remained facing her. She turned to her left and took a step away from the creature. But before her weight had finished shifting, the dragonfly buzzed around her again. Circling her head twice, it stopped in front of her mask, waiting. It slowly flew back to the right, where it had been before, still facing Neela. She watched it, then took another step toward the flying being. It turned, flew a short distance, then turned back to her.

"Am I to follow you?" Neela's voice cracking from disuse.

The dragonfly bobbed in the air, waiting.

Neela reached into her pockets again. Releasing the clutched braid, she fingered through the various objects. When she touched the tiny pot, it was cold enough to bite. Gingerly, she removed the small bit of honey and offered it to the flying creature on her open palm.

The hooting sound rushed around her again, making

her jump and bones tinkle. Glancing around, she saw nothing but the odd foliage through her eye slits. Neela looked back at the dragonfly and saw it now held the small pot clasped with its legs. She could still feel the burning cold upon her palm where the pot had rested. She shook her hand and shoved it back into her pocket, searching for the reassurance of the braid, and nodded at her new guide.

The dragonfly bobbed once more and turned. It flew, darting, then pausing, to make sure Neela was following, leading her past trees whose gnarled trunks were wider than she was tall. It wove among black and red vines which dripped down from the thick intertwining canopy above. More of the glowing firefly-like orbs bobbed around the foliage, their different colored lights twinkling as they flitted in and out of the leaves.

Neela's muscles ached from so much walking. She had not been immune to the Withering, and she had spent much of her time in huddled research when not tending to her grandmother. Her breathing had become labored when she lost sight of the dragonfly as it darted behind an enormous tree.

Rounding the tree, she discovered a glade with a large stump near the middle. The bushes grew low around the edges and the mists thinned enough to see patches of the ground beneath. The dragonfly hovered in the middle of the clearing, waiting for her.

As Neela approached it, she realized what she had mistaken for a stump was an enormous owl. Gripping a fallen branch, the being was as tall as Neela. Its wing and back feathers were a dark smoke color, streaked with the glowing snail slime the tree trunks had. Its breast was pale and spotted with complete blackness. The spots had a depth to them, as if they were small tunnels of night calling out to be explored.

The great owl ruffled its feathers, and the dragonfly bolted, leaving Neela to stand alone before it. It watched her with deep, orange-red eyes, pupils the same depth as its breast spots.

Neela's bones clinked as she shook off the entrancement the owl's eyes offered and began fingering her objects again. Two objects felt cold this time, the seven-pointed bronze star, and the carved wooden bead.

The bead belonged to her grandmother, gifted by an admirer in her youth. Carved into the shape of an owl's head, her grandmother had kept it wrapped in a soft cloth, worn tucked into her waistband, until her skirt was too loose to stay put. She had insisted Neela take it with her.

Neela offered the objects to the great owl spirit. The owl ruffled again, then shot one wing out and swept it over Neela's trembling palm. It resettled and waited.

Neela bowed low. "Great Spirit of the Underland, I seek aid for my people. They are dying from lack of nourishment and cannot gain it with food nor water. Even the animals wither and die. How can I help them?"

There was a slight rustling, followed by a chorus of hums. Then silence.

Neela waited for ten breaths, then looked up. There was no sign of the owl. In its place floated three of the glowing firefly-like beings. Stepping closer, she saw they were not insects, but pulsing spheres of light, the size of fat plums.

A deep voice rumbled through the clearing, running up through her feet and shaking her mask bones.

"CHOOSE ONE."

Neela gulped and bent close to examine the orbs. Their centers flickered like the flame of a candle, but each pulsed with a different color. The left one was a deep purple, the middle a pale green, and the last a brilliant orange.

She tried fingering the remaining objects in her pocket, but they gave no clues. This was to be her choice alone. She wished she knew what she was choosing.

Neela held her hand close to each one and felt a slight warmth emanating from the orange one. She grasped it gently, and it buzzed as its glow pulsed through her skin, making her hand feel its lost strength again. She stood mesmerized before remembering she needed to find her way back out.

Reaching the place she had stepped into the owl's clearing, she looked around. The thick mists made her unsure of which direction she should try.

A small squeak from near her feet caused her bones to tinkle again. A dull brown rat the size of a cat sat back on its haunches, staring up at her.

Neela took a half-step back.

The rat stayed still, waiting.

"H-hello. Will you guide me out?"

The enormous rat made another tiny squeak and waited.

Neela felt through her pockets and discovered the

small bag of barley was warm, not cold. She pulled it out and dangled it by its drawstrings. "Will this work as payment?"

The rat's tail and whiskers twitched as it reached up.

Neela lowered the gift into its grasp. The rat clutched the bag with its sharp teeth and turned into the mist.

She followed.

The ground mists often obscured the rodent, but the being would make occasional jumps, breaking the surface of the gray clouds to mark the way.

Neela was well worn by the time they reached the tunnel entrance. The rat waited a few feet inside as she caught her breath.

When the rat squeaked twice, Neela nodded. "Yes, I'm ready."

The soft orange glow of the globe was of little help to illuminate the pitch-black tunnel. She kept the barest touch upon the scarred wall as she followed the squeaks of the rat, stepping with care over the bumpy floor, until the dim light of the vestibule appeared ahead. Her steps became more sure as the passage floor evened out, and she caught the loping silhouette of the rat ahead of her.

Her trip had been less perilous than most of the recollections she had studied. But, had she chosen correctly? Whatever the orange sphere was, she hoped it would be of help to her people.

As she stepped into the open space of the vestibule, she noticed all but one passage, the unmarked entrance tunnel, was sealed with either rock or immense wooden doors. She glanced around, but could not see her rat guide anywhere.

She moved toward the passage, her exit from this strange world, but before she stepped inside, her first chicosk guide reappeared from the tunnel's depths, blocking her path. Neela's bones jingled with her sudden stop. Looking up at its melting mask, it appeared more ominous than before.

The being seemed fixated on the globe held in her hand.

Keeping a tight grip on the globe, she rummaged through the remaining items in her pockets again. When she touched the silver coin, its cold made her gasp.

Pulling it out with her free hand, she offered it to the chicosk.

"I—I'm ready to leave, now." Her voice quivered a little.

The chicosk had followed the movement of her hand which held the sphere. Now, it tilted its head toward Neela's face, and after a moment's hesitation, took the proffered coin.

It turned and started down the passage, its glow not as bright as before. Neela followed, eager to free herself of the Underland.

As the dark of the tunnel closed in around her, she heard a soft squeak. Neela glanced over her shoulder. The opening of the vestibule was a distant, dim spot the size of her thumb. As she turned back, the chicosk's glow ceased.

Neela froze as her eyes sought the warm glow of the globe clutched in her hand. It was faint now. Fainter than in the previous passage.

Something brushed past her, and a wave of goosebumps ran through her entire body, causing her to shudder. Her pulse pounded in her ears and her bones tinkled faintly as they settled from the movement.

She felt a slight breeze against the back of her neck before something grabbed her around the waist and threw her against the wall, face first.

Her mask protected her head, but she heard it crack. She slumped to the sandy floor, her whole body shaking from the impact. Still gripping the sphere, she held it up before her to see her attacker.

It was the first chicosk guide. It bent down over her, the pale orange light reflecting eerily over the rippled folds of its mask.

Neela pulled her knees close into her body and coughed. "Why?"

The chicosk raised its arm, poised to strike.

Neela felt her strength waning from the collision with the wall and so, *so* much walking. The sphere pulsed in her hand, its warmth comforting. On instinct, she thrust it toward the chicosk's eyes and it emitted a brilliant blinding light. She drew her other arm up to shield her own eyes and heard the chicosk stumble back, slamming into the opposite wall.

The squeak came again and Neela shivered as the rat guide brushed past her folded legs. It turned toward her in the fading orange light and gave two quick squeaks.

Neela struggled to her feet. The moment she was up, the rat ran. She stumbled after it, guided by its cries in the dark, her left hand brushing the wall reliefs to steady herself. Clutched in her right hand, the globe flickered as if about to go out.

A distant scrapping sounded behind her spurred her to move faster, but the ashy sand pulled at her feet.

A small light grew in the distance ahead. Her way out.

She pushed her shaky legs onward, trying to gain ground ahead of the approaching scrapes. Her head pounded, her ribs hurt, and bruises throbbed everywhere. She knew she would not heal from this. Her only slim chance was to break free from the Underland with the sphere. She was uncertain of what would happen then.

The scraping grew near and the rat ran back past her, squeaking wildly. It turned and nipped at her heels, urging speed.

The light from the entrance had grown enough Neela could see where the soft ground became more solid. She pushed herself to a stumbling run.

The air changed, becoming fresher as she neared the light. Sounds of life echoed dimly from outside.

Just as she reached the entrance, something caught her leg. It pulled her back and down, slamming her to the ground hard. Air burst from her lungs.

The chicosk rolled her onto her back, pinning the hand clutching the orb, and punched her mask hard.

A crack echoed in the entrance, and the scattered bird song of the outer world ended.

A chunk of Neela's mask broke off, revealing one violet eye.

Her vision split between the vision of the mask and the sight of her own world.

The sphere pulsed in her hand. She saw the chicosk preparing to strike again.

With her free hand, she reached up and grasped the chicosk's dangling skeleton, and yanked hard. The bones came free and disintegrated in her clenched fist. The chicosk released her hand clutching the throbbing orb and Neela drove it into the right eye hole of the chicosk's mask.

The chicosk stumbled back, emitting a piercing squeal.

The glowing globe melted into the mask and light shot out of both eye slits.

Neela drug herself backward with her elbows, watching the chicosk scrabble at the mask, trying to free itself of the light. It collapsed to its knees, and the mask fell away, revealing the face of King Jaluduth.

Neela blinked. She could see his face clearly with both her masked eye and her free one. It was her king. His face was not half melted like the mask. Instead, a heavy growth of beard sparsely covered deep scars across the right side of his face.

Her masked eye saw the king's face upon the dark spindly body of the chicosk. Her free eye saw the king in his own body, but his skin was soot black and rippled under tattered clothing.

The king gasped and squeezed his eyes shut. When he opened them, their whites kept a soft orange glow around his deep brown irises. He glanced out of the Underland's entrance, then focused on Neela.

"You...you are from my city?" the king asked.

Neela nodded, pulling herself closer to the wall and closer to the entrance.

"You worked with the polymaths, didn't you? Did you come to the Underland seeking an end to the Withering?"

Neela nodded again.

The king closed his eyes, then his left shoulder twitched violently. When it stopped, he said in a strained voice, "I, too, came. I know not how long ago. But, this *thing* consumed me."

Neela's masked eye could not help but stare at the chicosk body.

The king caught the slight movement of her mask and shook his head. "No. This is not one of the chicosk. It is one of the others. It holds my flesh captive and fed off my mind and emotions until it ripped my soul from me." He looked at Neela, the orange glow of his eyes softly pulsing. "You must have returned it."

Neela tried to sit up straight, but the soreness and pains crumpled her back against the stone. "I was offered a choice of three spheres, your highness. I did not know one of them was you."

"I am grateful nevertheless," the king said. "What is your name?"

"Neela, your highness."

"Neela. I cannot break free from this thing, Neela. It has consumed too much of me. As I fought it, I learned it was the thing causing the Withering. It desires to be above with us. To feed off of us."

A grimace of pain flooded the king's features and his

left leg jutted out at an impossible angle. He gasped, then panted off the pain until he could speak again.

"It seeps a slow poison up into the roots of our crops so it can feed off of the thoughts of sorrow it creates. It grows stronger, every day." King Jaluduth paused, glancing out the entrance into the forest. "I do not think it is strong enough to survive out there yet, but it soon will be. I grieve for the sake of the world if that should happen."

Neela coughed, drawing the king's attention.

"Did it—we do that to you?"

Neela nodded.

The king met Neela's eyes and the orange of his own pulsed dully, fading.

"I am truly sorry," he said. "I cannot keep it back much longer."

Another pulse of pain shot across his face and he panted until he could speak again. "You...you must do something for me. For our land. It is much to ask, but you were brave enough to come to the Underland."

"W-what is it, my king?" Neela's voice trembled slightly.

"If you can, you must destroy us both to free our land of the Withering. I won't be able to hold it back much longer."

Neela gave a weak smile beneath her mask. She could barely move and the king—King Jaluduth himself—was asking her to kill him.

She shifted, trying to ease her pains. Her hand fell against something hard in her cloak pocket. Clenching her teeth, she wiggled her hand inside. Somehow, the small vial of wine was still intact. Poisoned wine. The vial felt warm as sunshine. She pulled it out and showed it to her king.

"This is violet wine, your highness," she said. "It...it is a very special wine. I believe you have a fondness for it?"

She watched the king's haggard face closely. Meeting his eyes, she nodded slowly.

"Yes, Neela," the king said, his left eyebrow cocking. "It has been a favored drink among royalty for centuries."

She knew then that the king understood. Violet wine had often been a last request of dying monarchs of the past, laced with things to make the rulers passing quick and relatively painless. She hoped the first would be true, but doubted the last.

"I offer it to you as a gift, your highness," she said. "To ease your pain and suffering."

She held the vial upon her quivering palm and extended her arm as much as she could.

The king nodded and pulled his twisted body toward her. He reached out, grasped the vial, and retreated. Panting from the effort, he looked toward the entrance of the Underland. They were but a few feet from the opening and the woods beyond.

"Thank you, Neela," He didn't look at her. "I shall drink it in the sunlight, I think."

Neela watched the king pull himself out of the tunnel, and prop himself against a tree facing away from the Underland. He convulsed once, nearly dropping the vial, then stilled enough to pull the cork and down the contents in one gulp.

A moment later, her masked eye saw the chicosk's many legs jerk and writhe. She turned away, wishing she could close her ears to their shrieks and the thumps of flailing limbs slamming into the tree trunk.

She coughed and cringed at the pain in her chest. She stared into the darkness of the Underland tunnel, taking shallow breaths as she waited for the sounds to end. Her eyes caught a slight movement in the darkness before her, and a shiver racked her, making her flinch.

The rat appeared a moment later, bounding toward her and stopping at her side. It rested back on its haunches and squeaked.

Neela's split vision showed a rat of two colors. The mask's eye showed the dull brown fur she remembered. Her own eye saw fur that shimmered like silver.

"Thank you." She tentatively placed her hand on its back. The fur was soft, like that of a well-fed cat, and she stroked it gently.

The rat moved closer, then hopped over Neela's legs and sprung out into the sunshine of the outer world. It turned and squeaked at her again.

"I have no strength, little one. I am broken and I will not mend."

It hopped toward her and back several times, finally stopping an arm's length away.

Neela looked out toward the tree the king had rested against. All was silent, and she saw a jumble of limbs, human and chicosk, in a tangled heap. The trunk hid the king's torso; the wood missing large chunks of bark up and down its surface. Traces of red glinted along the edges of the deep cuts.

Neela could smell the rich, clean scent of the forest. She closed her eyes, inhaling as deeply as she dared.

The rat squeaked again, and Neela reopened her eyes. The rat stood a short way out of the entrance, Sunlight shimmered on its fur and danced through the leaf shadows around the animal. She felt so cold now, and the sunlight was enticing.

"All right, little one. I will try."

Bending over, she gingerly lowered herself down to her elbows and pulled herself along the hard ground with them, her knees slipping as much as pushing her closer toward the rat. It wasn't far. The stone entrance was only a body length away and the patch of speckled sunlight only a bit more. But every inch filled her body with pain as the movement shifted her cracked ribs.

Her mask fell away completely as she cleared the entrance, but she did not dare stop until her nose nearly bumped into the rat. She stared at the glossy black eyes and silver coat with both of her own violet ones. It leaned in and touched her nose with its own, then bounded away a short distance.

The ground shuddered and Neela looked back at the Underland entrance. It had sealed itself with tall narrow stones like long moss-covered teeth.

Panting, Neela curled up on her side. Fingers shaking, she slid her hand into her cloak pocket one last time. Pulling the braid out, she clutched it with both hands.

"I am so tired. I shall sleep now." She smiled sadly at the rat. "Will you stay with me?"

The rat hopped in close, then circled until it laid in a small ball resting against Neela's chest. It stayed with her until Neela took her last shallow breath. Then, gently grasping the braid in its teeth, it bounded toward the city.

TALE 3
# VAPORS OF MISUSE

Purgath poked the prone man's cheek with his staff. He glanced at the young man's spirit-sister, Silvy, kneeling next to him. She was still here, so he knew Larrin wasn't dead, despite his appearance.

"You're running out of time, Silvy," Purgath said, his voice coarse with age, his words heavy as stone.

Silvy flinched a little, then glanced up at him, her spirit-form shimmering like moonlight on a muddy puddle. He was one of the few who retained enough essence to see her.

The old man said, "If Vyanna gains any more power, you won't be able to kill her."

Silvy's gaze dropped to Purgath's feet. He watched the girl's mouth moving, but the twins' fates were too close to the gates now, and her voice would not come to him.

The twins had been nine at the time of the ritual, and Silvy had kept the shape of the girl she had been. Larrin towered above her now when the two stood side-by-side. Purgath had never told Silvy she could change her shape to match her brother as he grew. Nurturing her frustrations seemed a more profitable endeavor.

Purgath tutted. "It's been five moons since I was last here, Silvy. I thought the deed would finally be done."

Silvy looked at her prone brother, balling her fists, lips still forming soundless words.

Larrin still had not moved, and no breath was detectable; but the spidery, gray web of the Seizing pulsed across his left forearm and at the base of his neck. It was much darker and more widespread than the last time Purgath had seen him. Time was truly running out.

Purgath kicked at Larrin's boot. "Did you Harvest another one?"

Silvy nodded, not looking up at him.

Purgath studied her. Silvy's own Seizing marks had nearly disappeared, sucked through the gates into her brother.

The old man grunted and tapped his staff on the ground. "I'll only be here through the gibbous. I will try to provide an opportunity, but if you fail, Silvy..."

She finally met his eyes and the irises that had once been the same blue as her brother's pulsed ember orange.

"He has no more time left. The Seizing will take him. Soon."

～

OUR PARENTS TOLD *Silvy and me about the great calamity, back when our people still lived in Betalla three generations ago.*

*The land had split, giving way under the weight of countless broken essences that had been shoved into the ground by a power hungry Elite, shedding what they believed to be useless. A gapping maw grew, spewing the tattered and twisted essences back up into the air. They randomly attached themselves to the citizens of Betalla, Seizing them. Feeding off of them.*

*The most powerful Elites deserted us, leaving those who were sick and dying behind. Trying to save themselves and their powers. The citizens who remained moved to form a new colony, Betilard, pressed against the towering cliffs of Ilke and the sheer drop to the thermal seas of Ardwin. There they stayed, as far away from the maw as they could, watching people continue to die. Slowly trying to rebuild their lives.*

*A few of the lowest Elites had stayed behind. Those with ill families. Those who once believed the Seizing to be temporary. Once they had lost those they loved, they dedicated themselves to wiping each other out, claiming each other's essences, until the strongest one became our "leader".*

*Vyanna, The Wise One.*

*Our mortal enemy.*

THE PALE DAWN was breaking through the damp branches when Larrin's eyelids fluttered. Silvy grasped his hand, giving the slightest pressure until his eyes stayed open.

"You were out a long time," Silvy said, her eyes glistening.

Larrin focused on his twin's face. She looked just as she had sixteen years ago, just in different shades. The same high ponytail and small oval face. The same frailness from lack of food and proper care.

He looked nothing like himself at that age. But there was nothing left of that boy.

"I'm sorry I worried you." Larrin raised his aching arm and brushed Silvy's cheek. It had taken a while to learn how to touch each other and not just pass through. But now, it was almost real.

A sad smile graced her face, and she cupped his hand in both of hers. "Purgath was here."

Larrin scowled. "Did he ask for the Harvest?"

Silvy shook her head. "No. He asked if we had done one."

Larrin closed his eyes. "I suppose he would with me looking like this. How long was I out?"

"A day and a night."

Larrin's eye flew open at that. "So long? No wonder you were worried."

Silvy released his hand and stared at the pulsing marks on his forearm. "We don't have much time left, Larrin."

With a heavy sigh, Larrin rolled to his side and pushed himself up. He staggered slightly as he stood, then rolled his shoulders. "I know. I suppose Purgath was disappointed?"

Silvy sighed. "He can't hear me anymore, so I couldn't argue about it."

"It's fine." His neck popped as he rolled his head. "I've only got the strength for a few more Harvests, anyway. Was he coming back?"

"Purgath said he'd be here through the gibbous. He —" She paused, and her brother turned to look at her. "He said he would try to create an opportunity."

Larrin's pale blue eyes flashed dark for an instant, then he nodded. "We should head back."

"You should eat something," Silvy said, moving to stand next to him.

Her twin shook his head. "I'm not hungry anymore, Silvy."

She looked so shaken, he reached out his hand. "Come on. Let's just get this done."

Silvy took his hand, climbed up onto his back, and they returned to the edge of Betilard.

*Most citizens* of Betalla had some kind of essence blessing. Simple, everyday things that didn't require a chant or rite. A little extra strength when you needed it, knowing where to find a lost thing, better cooking or farming, the ability to heal yourself or assist others. Things that simply existed as a part of who each person was.

*The Seizing was drawn to all of it, powerful or not. Corrupting the blessing until it became toxic, often killing the host. Many of the people with the least amount of essence survived. For once their essence was destroyed, they still had enough of themselves left to heal from the Seizing. Eventually.*

*Not the kind of thing an Elite wants to know. That the*

*lowest class is the strongest. And the cost of survival was to lose their blessings. All essences. All power.*

*Measures were taken.*

THE TWINS SKIRTED the edge of the colony until they came to the path which led to their home. Hardly more than a sturdy lean-to, with mud and leaves daubed halfway up the sides to keep out the damp of the sea mists. It stood at the back of a ramshackle storehouse, one of the first built in the new colony. Now it stored things no one knew what to do with. Sometimes, even the dead.

From their doorway, they could see their former home, just over a short, wooded rise. Once the home of their parents. One of Vyanna's supporters had taken it after their deaths, leaving the twins to the wilds. It's why they had stayed here at the edge of Betilard. So they wouldn't forget.

Larrin lifted the woven door covering and slipped inside. While Silvy kept watch outside, he moved a small, lop-sided table and folded back the thread-bare rug, revealing a wooden box set into the ground.

He removed the lid and slipped an oval vial from a concealed pocket of his pants, nestling it beside the others in the box. The new vial glowed much brighter than the rest.

Living this far from the maw, it took strong winds to carry the cursed tendrils against the constant breezes from the Ardwin seas and into the colony. Nearly two-thirds of the inhabitants no longer had any essence to attach to, and all had learned to read when the winds changed for ill. Those left susceptible hid in pits, or in the case of Vyanna and her minions, cellars stocked with all they might wish during their confinement.

Most deaths now were from old age or ill health and hardship. This vial's Harvesting had been of a middling Elite, one of the last who still possessed enough magic to make the risks of a Harvest worthwhile.

Returning the box and its coverings, Larrin examined the webbed lines on his left arm. It had crept further, nearly to his wrist while he had lain unconscious. He grimaced and clenched his fist to watch the lines sharpen and pulse. No, he did not have much time left.

"Larrin?"

He turned. Silvy was standing inside the doorway, gesturing for him to come to her.

He reached the door and peeked along the edge of its covering. Warmth faded from his fingers as his gaze landed on Vyanna, the hood of her purple cloak folded down, revealing her bone white hair. A small entourage accompanied her as they entered Larrin and Silvy's former home.

"What do you think they are doing?" Silvy asked.

Larrin shrugged. "It doesn't matter. There are too many people with her for it to concern us."

*OUR FAMILY WERE HARVESTERS. One of only three houses capable; all grew to be despised, our blessings mislabeled. We*

*were often called Reapers, as if we were the ones causing death.*

*When a citizen dies, or is nearly dead, the blessing of their essence can be removed and stored, to be given to another. Long ago, Harvesters stored these until they were needed to recover from illnesses or strengthen the rest of the deceased's family. But rumors and myths always exist around rituals of death.*

*They were rumors the remaining Elites propagated.*

AFTER MUCH NAGGING, Larrin agreed to make a small meal. The talon roots that grew plentifully near the sea cliffs cooked down into a palatable mush, and cost nothing, as long as no one saw you gather them. With no appetite, his bites were slow, but Silvy continued to push him to take just one more.

Her cajoling stopped when several muffled voices drew near. The noise dropped to whispers just outside their door.

Larrin cocked an eyebrow at Silvy, then set his bowl down and rose, just as someone called out.

"In the hovel. Are you there, boy?"

Larrin froze, recognizing the voice of Vyanna's third, Raedon. Shaking himself, he stepped forward and pulled open the door hanging.

There were five other than Vyanna and Raedon. He recognized them all, of course. None but Raedon seemed willing to look at him.

"The Wise One wishes to bestow a greeting to you, one of Betilard's Unfortunates."

Over the years, he'd gotten use to not reacting to Vyanna, or her minions, and never directly met their gazes. He knew that she, at least, remembered who he was and what she had done, but it was one of so many atrocities, it seemed to hold no meaning for her.

"Step forward, boy," Raedon said, his voice edged in annoyance.

Larrin did as asked and took one long stride to loom over Raedon's smaller stature. But he kept his eyes down, submissive.

Raedon took a step back, exhaling through his nose.

A chuckle emanated from Vyanna as she stepped forward.

Larrin could feel Silvy peeking from their doorway. He'd never been sure if Vyanna could see her. It took a strong connection to her, or a lot of held essence. Vyanna had been collecting Harvests for a long time, but she never gave any indication of seeing his spirit-sister. Maybe she thought *he* couldn't.

Vyanna placed cold, fleshy fingers upon his chin and raised it to peer up into his eyes. She studied his face for a moment, then grabbed his left wrist and stretched his arm toward her. Larrin resisted the urge to react. He didn't have the strength to end her now. Even with the strength of all the Harvests they had saved, he wasn't sure he could; but he knew he must try… soon.

"You've had these marks a long time, Marron."

"It's Larrin, Wise One." It was a game of hers, he

knew. Even so, he wanted her to remember the name of the one who would kill her.

Vyanna nodded absently, turning his wrist this way and that.

"It grows dark." She met his eyes and her lips hinted at a smile. "Your time grows short."

"Perhaps, Wise One."

He knew she could tell he still held some level of essence and was eager to collect it for her own.

He also knew she had no idea how much.

She dropped his wrist and glanced disparagingly at the hovel behind him.

"I've heard there's work available hauling the sea plants. You look like you've still got the strength for that, boy. It should be worth a meal or two."

Larrin obediently bowed slightly. "Thank you, Wise One."

She turned and walked away, her minions following.

*When our colony was forming and the few remaining Elites were busy fighting for power, they began raiding the Harvesters to gain additional stores of essences. The fewer Elites, the more they raided, until they decided it would be beneficial to cut the supply.*

*First one Harvester family was slaughtered, then the other. Until our house was the only one left.*

Silvy sat in the middle of the floor, silent, her arms wrapped around her knees.

Unfortunates. The word always stung her more than Larrin. But, at nearly twenty-five, "boy" did bother him.

Vyanna and her supporters had spread rumors about their parents and how they had died. They had been dangerous. Practicing forbidden and heinous rituals on the dead. Out to disrupt the precious balance Vyanna and the others were trying to maintain.

Foolish, since Betilard had mostly settled itself before the Elites' true battle for power had begun. The colony, once struggling to survive each day, had learned the wind patterns and how to avoid the tendrils of Seizing. They'd found ways to keep themselves fed and keep order, without the aid of the everyday blessings they once had. They hadn't needed an Elite to rule them.

But the stories had kept the twins as outcasts as young children. Untrusted. Unfortunate. And although a few took pity on Larrin when Silvy died, no one would offer him a proper job.

There had been other Unfortunates. Orphans from other families wiped out during the feuds, though no others of Harvester descent. Larrin knew of only two who had survived as long as he. One had gone mad after losing his blessing, and lived in a cave halfway up the Ilke. The other was taken in as a mistress to one of Vyanna's followers.

Purgath had been the only one to offer the twins assistance regularly.

He lived as a hermit at the base of the Ilke, far from

the colony and too close to the maw for anyone to want to visit him. Or attack him.

Larrin thought Silvy had grown fond of him.

He knew better.

Larrin tilted their small water bucket over a chipped cup, watching the last drops fall. "We're out of water. I'll go to the well. Please guard the house. I don't know if Purgath will come by."

Silvy shot a glare at him. "He's never taken any of the Harvests without asking for them."

"We're out of time, Silvy. We don't know what he's willing to do to prevent Vyanna from taking them."

Silvy scowled, then stared at her feet, brows drawn together in a furious pout.

Grabbing the water bucket, Larrin left Silvy to her grumblings. He avoided the main paths simply to steer clear of most people. The citizens weren't outwardly unkind. But now that his Seizing marks were more prominent, no one wanted to get too close. It was a reminder of all the lives lost.

The well was deserted this time of day, and Larrin set his bucket down before lifting the wooden cover off the stone walled shaft. Lowering the copper drawing bucket, he heard soft footsteps approaching from behind.

Purgath leaned in and set a folded scrap of paper onto the wall of the well.

"It will happen tonight. Be ready."

*WE WERE six when our parents were killed; believed to be too young to know anything of the ritual. That was partly true. But we were not too young to become consumed by vengeance. When Purgath arrived a year later, saying he had known our parents and knew of the ritual, we did everything he asked.*

IT TOOK both Larrin and Silvy to perform a Harvesting rite. One on each side of the gate. When the person wasn't dead yet, Silvy pulled them just close enough to unlock their essence. When they had just passed, she pushed a part of them back to allow the release of it. Meanwhile, Larrin would chant the Release to coax the essence away from its host, and toward the oval vial.

Occasionally, the dead or dying did not want to release their blessing. That had only happened twice for the twins. The second time they had ever performed the ritual, and their most recent one. It was why Larrin had been unconscious for so long.

That one had been on a long-suffering Seizing. Vyanna's second, Millian, had fought it for over five years. Other than himself, Larrin had only heard of one other Seizing lasting longer. Vyanna's original second had lived with it for almost nine years.

Larrin knew it annoyed Vyanna that she hadn't been able to get there soon enough to collect Millian's essence herself. But the winds had shifted a little that day and Vyanna and her minions had taken to their cellars, just in case. She thought Millian's essence had passed away, unharvested.

The thought made Larrin smile.

*THERE ARE two rituals for Harvesters. The one we knew about was the actual Harvesting of the essences. We had seen our parents perform it and were learning the basics before they were killed. But in order to perform this ritual—repeatedly, over the years, without harming oneself or the essences—one has to survive another ritual. One our parents had not mentioned. A blood ritual that required a twin.*

THE NIGHT PURGATH performed the ritual on the twins to become true Harvesters, he failed to mention that losing one of their lives was inherent to the rite. During the ceremony, the winds from the Ardwin suddenly changed, and the maw sensed it. When a tendril wrapped itself around them both just as Silvy's body fell, Purgath thought for sure all his plans would be lost, but the girl pulled most of the Seizing with her and only left a small faint mark on her brother. They were forever bound with it now; at least until the living one died. Slowly, the Seizing had bled through their connection over the years, pulling Larrin closer to the gate. Slowly closing Purgath's opportunities.

*THERE HAD BEEN a reason for three Harvester houses. You could marry between them and keep the blessings strong. Most couples had multiple sets of twins so the marriages could continue. Our parents were young and Silvy and I were their only ones.*

~

LARRIN PLACED ALL the vials in his pockets, then flipped the rug back into place.

Silvy gave him an uncomfortable look. "Are you sure?"

"It might be our last chance."

They left their shack, Silvy riding Larrin's back, and made their way to the house written on Purgath's slip of paper.

A rumble of voices caught their attention as they neared. At least a dozen people stood in front of the house, huddled in two's and three's, some exclaiming and waving their arms, some whispering, wringing their hands.

Silvy tapped her twin's shoulder and pointed.

Purgath was slipping behind the next building over, away from the small crowd.

The twins veered to the side of the house, away from the noise, to a side door. They peeked around the back of the house, but saw no signs of Purgath.

Stepping back to the doorway, Larrin pulled the heavy mat hanging aside, and Silvy slid down from her brother to peer in. She waved at him and he stepped inside. The larger homes were built with maze-like passages to break the path of any winds. Warily, Larrin made his way through the house's hallways, Silvy keeping guard behind. They paused at the doorway of the sleeping chamber, listening. Only one sound could be heard; the rough, labored breathing of an older man.

Larrin signaled Silvy, and she moved in until she was next to the bed.

"Larrin."

He took one last look down the hallways before moving in beside her. The man was Liddeo, the representative of the workers to Vyanna's council. He had been always extremely careful about avoiding the tendrils, and he would have taken to shelter during the last wind shift.

"I see no marks," Silvy said.

Larrin leaned close to the old man, examining his arms, then his neck. When he neared the man's whiskered chin, he took an abrupt step back and covered his mouth.

"What is it?"

"It's not the Seizing," Larrin whispered to her. "He's been poisoned."

The man's lips and eyelids were turning a purply blue and his breaths were becoming infrequent.

"I don't like this, Silvy. He's not got long to live."

"Purgath?" Silvy asked.

Larrin gave a slight shrug.

Silvy stared at the dying man. "Will it be enough?"

Larrin looked at his sister for a moment. She seemed...eager. "Perhaps."

"Then we must take it."

Larrin took another step back and ran a hand through his short, dark hair. "Purgath said he would create an opportunity. How does this get us closer to Vyanna?"

Silvy tilted her head. "It's more for us to use against her."

"You know the toll it's taking on me now, Silvy. I won't be in any condition to use it for a few days at the rate I'm going. If I even awake from it."

Silvy looked at him, anger flashing in her orange eyes. "What else are we supposed to do? Purgath led us here and there is essence to Harvest."

Larrin took another step back, shaking his head. "I don't know what Purgath wanted, but I don't think it was for us to Harvest."

Before Silvy could argue, the voices from outside rumbled into the house.

I'M sure Purgath knew the cost to us. Sometimes I wonder if Silvy knew. If he told her, and she had still agreed. He must have known I would not.

VYANNA'S VOICE rose above the rest. It echoed around the passageways.

"I will check on him. Raedon said he is not long for this world. I would be with him at the end."

Orange eyes met blue, and the twins heard the heavy

flapping of a door mat, muting the voices of many, and leaving the footsteps of one.

There was no time to leave the room without risking being seen, and few places to hide inside the sparse space. A window hung to the right of the small bed, but it was narrow and would take time for Larrin to shove himself through.

Silvy hissed and pointed to the corner to the right of the door. A tall wooden chest stood there, a cherished remnant of Betalla days, with carved feet and handles. It stood a shoulder-width away from the corner. Larrin looked at the corner doubtfully but could find nowhere else to go.

Wedging himself against the wall, he squatted down and began taking slow, measured breaths.

Silvy merged into the wooden chest. She didn't like being inside things. It made her feel less real, but she could move through its edges to watch what Vyanna did.

A moment later, Vyanna stepped into the room. She did not look anywhere but the bed, and at the dying man upon it. Larrin lost sight of her as she strode forward. Her footsteps paused and her robe rustled.

"You really aren't long for this world, are you, Liddeo?" Vyanna's voice lacked compassion but held an edge of curiosity. "What is it that's killing you? It can't be the Seizing."

A moment later, Vyanna gasped, and Larrin heard her feet shuffle.

"Poison? But who would want to upset the balance?" She sighed. "I worked so hard for your position, Liddeo. This is very inconvenient."

Her feet shuffled again.

"Well, at least it will not be all in vain. You have enough essence to make the risk worthwhile."

*THERE HAVE ALWAYS BEEN a few Elites who could perform a Harvesting, it just costs them. A trade. Part of the essence they are collecting. Part of their own.*

VYANNA BEGAN THE RITUAL CHANT, a melodic rhythm to steps she took back and forth around Liddeo's bed.

Silvy's face emerged from the chest next to Larrin, the wood grain distorting her dusky features. She kept her voice a whisper, just in case Vyanna could hear her. "What do we do?"

Larrin closed his eyes for a moment, listening. It was the long, older version of the chant they knew. They would have time. Quietly, he pulled the vials out of his pockets.

Silvy drew a hand out from the chest and tapped his shoulder. "Are you sure?"

Larrin mouthed, "Opportunity."

Vyanna's chanting filled the room, and her steps began a pulsing buzz Larrin could feel through the woven floor mats. She was stronger than Larrin had guessed.

Silvy merged back into the chest, then returned quickly. "Purgath is outside the window."

A glimmer flickered in Larrin's eyes. Silvy's brow furrowed.

As quietly as he could, Larrin grasped the vials in both hands and began reciting their Release in his head, lips silently tracing the words. He hoped Vyanna's pulses would cover the essence shifts he was creating.

The power of the vials moved into his palms and caused his hands to glow.

Vyanna's chanting slowed for a few heartbeats, then returned to its normal cadence.

Larrin quietly returned each vial to his pockets and reached inside his shirt to pull a larger, empty vial from a cord around his neck. He met his sister's eyes.

Silvy glanced toward Vyanna's voice, then back to her brother. She nodded once and her youthful face took on a sternness Larrin had never seen before. Her hand reached out and she grasped the vial. She met Larrin's eyes and together they mouthed the Release. The Release of all the power Larrin had stored in his spirit-sister.

*I know now that Purgath has used us to try and take Vyanna down. He wants her power for himself.*

Silvy's hand glowed the same ember-orange of her eyes. When she released the vial, it shone like a small, vibrant star, and Silvy's eyes dulled to a faint black-brown.

Vyanna's chanting had slowed again, as did her footsteps. But stopping the ritual now would mean having to start over again.

Silvy pulled back into the chest. A moment later Vyanna's chanting and footsteps continued, and Silvy appeared to Larrin again. Pulling most of her torso away from the wooden box, she reached her twin's ear. With the barest breath, she said, "She's confused. She can feel something. She glances at the doorway and window but doesn't stop moving. I don't see Purgath outside, but I don't think he's gone far."

Larrin's eyes were closed, his fist wrapped tightly around the glowing vial, its essences slowly pulsing into him. When they had first begun Harvesting, they had made many mistakes. Small bits of essence would escape or not be powerful enough to warrant a vial. Silvy had tried to catch them on the other side and keep them there. Sometimes, bits of the Seizing would get broken off and mixed with the pieces of whole essence. Silvy collected those, too.

When Purgath began taking the most powerful of vials as payment for his aid, the twins began storing more away from his grasp. How else would they have enough power to slay the one responsible for their family's annihilation?

Larrin nodded and mouthed, "When I'm full, we'll begin."

THE CLOSER *I draw to my end, the less I seem to care about Vyanna herself. I just want this to be done.*

∾

LARRIN OPENED HIS EYES. A vibrant golden-orange displacing the blue. He released the vial in his hand and it dropped to his chest, dull and empty. The Seizing marks of his neck had grown up to grace his jawline and the ones of his arm traced their way down to his finger-tips. He shivered from their increased potency, feeding off the massive uptake of essences.

He listened to where Vyanna was in her chant. They had almost taken too long. She only had a few more lines to recite.

He nodded at Silvy, and she nodded back.

He rose slowly, peering over the chest. Vyanna's back was toward him. He took a soft step forward and Silvy stepped free of the chest to stand beside him.

Vyanna's arms were raised, an intricate chain of pale light strung between her fingers. She stepped to the side of the small bed, her back still to the twins, and lowered her web to just above Liddeo's throat. The man was a breath away from death, his skin now splotched purple.

One more line and the ritual would be in motion.

A slight movement caught Larrin's attention. The very edge of Purgath's robe fluttered at the side of the window's opening.

A thought stirred, but Larrin forced his attention back to his fate.

On quiet feet, Larrin stepped behind Vyanna, raising his hands to his chest, palms out. She stiffened, her hands halting their downward movement, her tongue freezing on the last four words.

Silvy slipped in front of Vyanna, to stand in front of her, passing through the dying man and his bed. She faced the Wise One and gave her a ghoulish smile.

Vyanna gasped. Spinning around, she met Larrin's glowing eyes. The web of light she held extinguished and a glare of hatred bore into him.

Larrin took a quick, deep breath, and shoved his palms into Vyanna's chest, just below her collarbone. Exhaling, he pushed all the pieces of Seizing Silvy had collected into her. Then drove them deep with the strength of their other gathered essences.

Vyanna shuddered and grabbed Larrin's wrists, trying to wrench them away from her. Then she growled and her power filled her hands with a glowing red rage.

Larrin grimaced as a hot pain filled his arms, but he did not stop. He stepped into her instead, forcing her against the edge of the bed and sliding her toward the wall.

The corner of Vyanna's mouth lifted. She spat through gritted teeth. "Good. Nice and strong. I will take that blessing of yours, just like your parents."

*I wish I had been the one to cross first. Or that we both had at the same time.*

THE SMELL of burnt hair and charred flesh filled the room

as Larrin's arms took the full brunt of Vyanna's rage. He pushed harder.

The dark Seizing marks of Larrin's fingers stretched into Vyanna's robe and crawled up her exposed flesh, heading for her throat.

Fragments of essence began splintering off from the clash, floating out into the room as color-tinged puffs of tangible smoke.

Silvy faded to the other side of the gate. She shoved Liddeo's essence away from the narrowly missed connection and felt his body die on the other side. The ritual chanting had brought Vyanna so close to the other side, Silvy could feel her essence strands still pulling toward Liddeo's.

Silvy reached out and chanted the Release, pulling.

My last breath *is coming soon, but I have vowed I will destroy her. For Silvy, if not for myself.*

Vyanna gasped, color draining from her face.

Her grip on Larrin's wrists lessened. She took a deep breath, then squeezed his burnt flesh harder. She met his eyes with cold fury. "Don't you realize how much power I have, boy? You, and whatever your little shade are doing, will never bring me down."

A different chant issued from her lips. Larrin did not know what she was trying to do. He had only known the ways of a Harvester and how to use the essences for Harvesting. And the pain, the blinding pain Vyanna was filling him with, was making it hard to think. But he could feel Silvy's connection pulling at Vyanna's essences through the gate.

From the corner of his eye, Larrin caught a flash of movement from the window. Purgath was up to something, but he needed to focus.

~

*COULD we take them both down?*

~

SILVY FELT the raw power of the essences as she drew on Vyanna, as well as the shattered bits welded together into strange and potent things. Some were damaged and beast-like, angered at being used and imprisoned; a side effect of the trade an Elite offered to Harvest. They were held together with bits of the Elite's own essence. Silvy could tell some belonged to Vyanna, but others... perhaps they were from other Elites Vyanna had stolen from?

She tried to soothe them as she untangled what she could. Thin threads of the Seizing were also scattered throughout, nearly hidden. She pulled those aside, as she had always done, saving them for later.

Glowing with the amount of essence she had collected, she let go. Vyanna still held more, but Silvy had nowhere to keep it, and it was taking too much time.

Released from Silvy's pull, Vyanna shoved Larrin

hard. He fell to his knees, spent. The flesh of his arms charred past his elbows. His fingertips nearly burnt to the bone.

Vyanna braced herself against the wall, panting, oblivious to the webs of Seizing now running across her neck and up around her left ear.

"Fool!" she spat. "You've gone and wasted so much. It almost isn't worth Harvesting from you."

Silvy emerged from the other side, just behind Larrin, glowing like a brilliant flame. She wrapped her arms around him and her small hands found the empty vial around his neck. The essences she had stolen from Vyanna flowed into it; she kept only the stray strands of Seizing to herself.

She whispered to her brother, "Pull it in as fast as I Release it."

Larrin reached thin, blackened fingers up to the vial until they bumped into it; he could no longer feel the smooth glass.

"What are you doing now?" Vyanna tried righting herself, but swayed. She pointed a finger at Larrin. "If I kill him, you won't be able to cross anymore and you'll lose whatever power you think you have, spirit girl."

Silvy ignored Vyanna, continuing to let the essences fill Larrin's vial as fast as she could, but her eyes were drawn to movement by the window.

*HAS Silvy grown too fond of Purgath, despite his deception? Or would she agree?*

PURGATH HAD REACHED his hand in through the narrow window and was sliding it against the wall. A pale light slithered out from his fingers toward the battle; an anti-shadow reaching for the stray essences spilling out into the room.

Finishing the Release, Silvy left her brother and passed through the wall to stand next to Purgath.

He started, his arm frozen inside the room.

"What do you want, spirit girl? Get back in there and destroy the one who killed your parents!"

Silvy frowned at him, wishing he could hear what she wanted to say. Then, the corners of her mouth descended into a deep scowl and she reached into his chest, placing her hands around his heart.

"I know you used us, Purgath. I am not as malleable as you think. You only wanted the power for yourself, without paying a price."

His eyes grew wide and his jaw dropped, finally hearing the spirit-girl again.

Silvy's scowl morphed into a maniacal smile as she freed all the strands of Seizing she had gathered and let them wrap themselves deep within the old man's body of stolen essences.

She removed her hands, turned, and moved back through the wall to rejoin her twin.

*I don't remember a time when we didn't live in fear. Less fear when our parents were alive, but it was always there.*

LARRIN CONTINUED to pull from the vial, his body trembling. He had never felt such strange, broken essences before. He would never have guessed Vyanna had taken so many. There were hundreds of fragments, joined and separate. Had she been collecting them since Betalla? Were all these broken, angry pieces what the high Elites had been pouring into the ground trying to protect themselves from the cost of the trade? Is that why the Maw had happened?

Vyanna couldn't have much of her own blessing left. Not with the cost so high for an Elite. Could he sense it? Were those the thin strands holding some of the essences together? Silvy must have untangled some of the free ones from it, the ones radiating memories of anger and fear, resentment and betrayal.

Traces of healing essences ran through his charred skin, bringing more movement into his hands and wrists. And then his nerves came back to life.

He sucked in a breath, his mind growing fuzzy again from the pain.

*Sometimes I wonder, if my essence is finally eaten away by the Seizing and I lived, would I still be able to see Silvy? Or would our connection be lost forever?*

Sᴡᴇᴀᴛ ᴡᴀs sʟɪᴅɪɴɢ down Vyanna's face. What had that spirit girl done to her? She'd had no idea that orphan boy still possessed a connection like that. Where had he gotten all that essence? Had he been saving it since childhood? How could someone so young perform Harvestings and still be alive?

She needed to finish him, before she lost any more power. She wasn't sure if she could take his now. He couldn't have much left. Such a waste. She could have used it for years.

She tried to pull herself upright again. No good. She still needed the wall to brace herself against. What had they done? She felt hollow from her expenditure.

The spirit girl was gone again. It made her nervous. She had glimpsed her a few times over the years, but thought she was just a ghost. She caught sight of those occasionally. Often in places of death, especially deaths she had caused.

There had been so much death after the Maw had opened. The colony needed a leader to keep the people strong and focused. A leader who kept the essences in line, strong, but away from the Seizing. She had been in control for over a decade now. Her rivals slain. Why were there those who still resisted?

She looked upon the Unfortunate slumped before her. She needed to take this boy down.

*I THINK Silvy is stronger than I am. She understands what we do more than I. How it all works. Perhaps it's from her connection to the other side.*

◇

PURGATH TRIED TO BREATHE, but it was as if he lay between two slabs of stone. The splintered tendrils of Seizing were wrapping themselves around his essences tightly, and seeping out to pattern his pale, wrinkled skin.

How could the spirit girl do this? To him? After all he'd done?

He never Harvested anyone. The risks were too great. The twins were born Harvesters. It was their rite. He wasn't an evil man. No one had wanted them. They would have died without him. He had known their parents. Bought or traded Harvests from them and the others.

He felt his knees give way, and he fell into the dirt, still fighting to suck in air.

◇

*I ALWAYS FEEL like I should protect her. Perhaps because she still looks like she's nine.*

◇

THERE. That one. And that one. Those essences belonged to Vyanna. Larrin kept those to himself, pulling them away from the others. Unburdening their chains, the freed essences felt wild and vengeful, and with the very thought of being used against their captor, they pulled Larrin up onto his knees. They would do whatever he asked.

He still had a chance to fulfill his vow.

~

*IF WE SUCCEED, I wonder what will happen?*

~

VYANNA STEADIED herself and took a step forward. The Seizing marks now ran up her cheekbones.

"Now you die, boy."

She raised both her hands toward him and took another step forward, chanting. It was low, almost a hum, the air buzzing around her. Her fingers glowed a pale yellow, and thin tendrils snaked toward each other, weaving a web.

Larrin's knees nearly buckled as he rose to stand, but he caught himself before he could fall. He wasn't sure what Vyanna was about to do, other than prepare for his death.

He raised his damaged arms and called to the waiting essences. He could barely control them, but he didn't want to.

He coaxed them, hinted they could feed themselves into the Seizing growing inside Vyanna. Giving it the strength to envelop her and make her pay for their imprisonment.

He took a step forward and thrust his hands into the middle of Vyanna's web.

The essences he held burst out, flaring bright as a falling star. The impact made Vyanna stagger back into the wall, her web breaking apart as her arms dropped to her sides.

She gasped, then laughed, recognizing the essences as ones the spirit girl had taken.

"You fool! You just gave me back all the power your twin worked so hard to pull from me!"

Larrin fell to his knees. "Not quite."

The smile on Vyanna's face froze as she finally noticed the Seizing marks spreading like fire down her arms and hands. Her eyes grew wide as she watched them grow fat and black, merging into a solid sheath of her imminent death.

Her scream was cut short as she fell to the ground.

Larrin collapsed next to her.

*WHAT WOULD it be like to live without blessings? To live without the fear of your essences being taken away.*

SILVY KNEELED down next to her brother and stroked away the beads of sweat from his brow.

He blinked up at her, trying to keep her in focus.

"Purgath?"

"He's taken care of."

Larrin tried to raise an eyebrow in question, but it was too much effort.

"How do you feel?"

Larrin wanted to laugh. "How do you think?"

"Do you have any essence left?"

Larrin felt inside for the embers of essence. The warmth of the healing essences was gone, leaving a dull throbbing throughout his worn body. There was still pain, but not as intense. Nothing else. Not even the essence of Harvesting. He shivered.

"I'm empty."

"Good."

He stared up into Silvy's eyes. They were the blue they had been when she was alive. The same blue as his. But the color of her skin was fading. "I—I don't understand."

"There's no Seizing left in you. Or in me. It's got nothing left to feed on."

Larrin stared at his twin intently. The webbed marks that had been fading on Silvy's skin were no longer there.

A sad smile graced Silvy's fading lips. "We're no longer Harvesters. You just need to heal."

And then she was gone.

*WHAT WILL the citizens of Betilard think of me now? An Unfortunate who took the life of their leader.*

*Vengeance was sweet, but already I miss you, Silvy. Will you wait for me? It may be a short wait.*

# ACKNOWLEDGMENTS

I hope you've enjoyed delving into some of my darker works.

I write in a wide variety of genres, and although I enjoy dipping into the dark, I'm not sure if I'm ready to live an entire novel of it.

But we shall see.

In the meantime, I shall dwell dark upon occasion and collect them here in this series of Dark Threads.

A special note of thanks to Dave Farland, Superstars Writing Seminar, Writers of the Future, Alicia Cay, Mandy Hanks, and my family, for their support and encouragement.

~Kat

# About the Author

**Kat Farrow** grew up chasing stories through sagebrush and sandstone in the Four Corners region of the western U.S. Now a multi-genre author, she writes tales that whisk readers into fantastical worlds, captivating mysteries, and heartwarming adventures for readers young and old.

Her fiction appears in anthologies such as Parliament of Wizards, The Librarian Reshelved, and the award winning Noncorporeal. Her debut children's novel, Bobbin and the Magic Thief, received awards, critical praise, and a fan following in 2023.

When she's not writing, Kat's usually in the garden (fighting weeds), curled up with a book, or commandeered by her feline overlords.

For more works and updates:
loreweaver.com

# Also by Kat Farrow

**Short Fiction**

The Bad Luck Bride (Space Brides, LLC)

Shadow Image (Noncorporeal)

Keeper of Stone and Memory (The Librarian Reshelved)

The Hag's Imp (Witches of a Certain Age)

A Flash of Fingers (Parliament of Wizards)

The Wash-O-Matic Mishap (Mistletoe Merriment)

A Patchwork Christmas (Happy Holiday Historicals)

**Children's Work**

Bobbin and the Magic Thief

Bobbin and the Stolen Thread (Forthcoming)

**Novels**

Everyday Witches: A Very Familiar Life (wt) (Forthcoming)